The Lost Empire of Koomba

A Magical World Awaits You

Read

THE SECRETS OF DROON

and coming soon

THE SECRETS OF DROON

— TONY ABBOTT —

The Lost Empire of Koomba

Illustrated by Royce Fitzgerald
Cover illustration by Tim Jessell

SCHOLASTIC INC.
New York Toronto London Auckland
Sydney Mexico City New Delhi Hong Kong

For Dolores

For more information about the continuing saga of Droon,
please visit Tony Abbott's website at
www.tonyabbottbooks.com

ISBN-13: 978-0-545-09883-0
ISBN-10: 0-545-09883-1

Text copyright © 2009 by Tony Abbott
Illustrations copyright © 2009 by Scholastic Inc.

12   11   10   9   8   7   6   5   4   3   2   9   10   11   12   13   14/0

Printed in the U.S.A.
First printing, October 2009

Contents

Contents

One

The Riddle in the Smoke

Crunch . . . crunch . . . slurp . . . crunch . . .

"Try to be quiet, Neal," whispered Julie. "You'll wake the Hinkles."

"Sorry," said Neal, licking his lips. "It's hard to resist free food."

Crunch . . . slurp . . .

Neal had plucked a ripe apple off the tree outside their friend Eric's bedroom window.

It was an hour before dawn, and Julie and Neal were high in the branches of the tree. Once they'd sneaked in Eric's window, they hoped to slip down to his basement without his parents seeing them.

Neal had woken Julie earlier to say that he'd dreamed of giant drifts of green snow. Green snow could mean only one thing.

They were being called back to Droon.

"Tell me again," whispered Neal. "Why aren't we using the door?"

"Because I unlocked the window yesterday when I pretended to be Eric," Julie said.

Julie had the power to change shape. She'd pretended to be Eric because he was trapped in Droon — and because she didn't want his parents to worry.

"The door would have been so much easier," Neal sighed.

"The Hinkles lock the door at night," said Julie, reaching for another branch. "Now, hush!"

As she drew closer to the window, Julie thought about how much she loved that tree. It was the same tree they had all gotten stuck in way back in kindergarten. Eric's mother had had to come rescue them.

If it hadn't been for the hour spent in those branches, Julie might not have become Eric's close friend. If she hadn't become his friend, she might not have been in his basement when the magical staircase to Droon was discovered. And if she'd never discovered Droon, she would certainly not have gained magical powers.

Magical powers!

That also happened in a tree.

But not this one.

It was high in the treetops of the Bangledorn Forest that Julie was scratched on the hand by a wicked creature called a wingwolf. The scratch had hurt at the time, but Julie later discovered that it had passed both wingwolf powers to her: She could fly and change her shape.

Crunch . . . crunch . . .

"It's a little sour," Neal said.

"And a little loud," said Julie. "Shhh!"

Pausing just below Eric's window, Julie wondered what she always wondered: Would her powers help them in Droon that day?

She hoped so, because Droon certainly needed help.

In a fierce attack directed at Galen the wizard, Eric had been poisoned by an ice dagger. That was bad enough. But the terrible moon dragon, Gethwing, had used Eric's illness to transform him into Prince

Ungast, a wicked boy sorcerer who joined Gethwing's Crown of Wizards, the greatest alliance of evil in the history of Droon.

Eric was still alive, deep inside Prince Ungast, but he was fading fast. Even worse was the fact that Gethwing's armies were gathering for a massive attack on Jaffa City.

Five days, Eric had told their friend Princess Keeah. *I can hold them off for five days. Bring me the Moon Medallion. It's the only way to save Droon. If you can't . . . then it's over.*

The Moon Medallion was a device of unspeakable power. Julie knew that plans were under way to bring it to Eric.

Pausing to steady herself, she looked out at their sleeping neighborhood. *I can hold them off.* Eric's words were brave, but she knew that he was locked in the greatest struggle of his life.

But there was something else preying on Julie's mind as she scanned the houses and streets. Only hours before, a trio of strange, silent creatures known as the Hunters had ascended the magic stairs. Now they were out there somewhere.

What were they hunting for? Or whom?

"Okay, one more branch," she whispered.

Reaching up to the top limb, Julie felt her fingers slip. "Owww!"

A twig flicked her hand, scratching it.

All at once, her breath caught in her throat. Her ears burned. Her heart thumped. Her head swam. "Neal, I —"

To stop everything spinning around her, she closed her eyes.

And she was no longer outside Eric's house. She was in a place filled with swirling purple smoke, a fog of violet so thick she could barely see.

A shape moved in the smoke. It was large and cloaked and stepped toward her awkwardly. The smoke parted, and she saw the figure's face.

It was Galen! His old features were dark. He seemed troubled, uncertain, and afraid.

He spoke in a whisper. ". . . stolen . . . no one . . . for a hundred years!"

"Galen?" Julie whispered.

A second shape now hovered behind him in the swirling smoke. "Wizard, come," it said. "It is time. . . ."

The wizard shook his head over and over. "Nooooooo —"

Was this the journey the wizard had told them he would soon be taking? Could the other figure be Anusa, Galen's genie friend, his guide on the journey? And if it was Anusa, then why was he so troubled?

A moment later, the purple smoke enshrouded both figures, and they were gone.

"Galen?" said Julie. "Galen —"

"The name is Neal!" said Neal. "And you're in my way!"

Suddenly, Julie was back in the apple tree.

"Oh, my gosh!" she said. "I just had a vision. I think Galen might be in danger. Neal, I have to warn him —"

"Ahem!" said a voice.

Julie looked up. Five feet away, leaning out the bedroom window, was Eric's mother, Mrs. Hinkle. "Just what do you two think you're doing out there?"

Neal sighed. "We are so busted."

Mrs. Hinkle frowned. "Get in here before you break your necks!"

She helped them through the window and into Eric's room. Then she

searched their faces and breathed out a long, slow breath. Her eyes pooled with tears.

"The forgetting spell," said Julie. "You remember, don't you?"

Mrs. Hinkle nodded slowly. "When I saw Eric's empty bed this morning, everything came back to me. I know your friend Keeah put a spell on me, but it faded. I know about Prince Ungast and that . . . dragon."

"Keeah said the power of love can break even the strongest spell," said Julie.

Mrs. Hinkle sat on the bed and buried her face in her hands. "Oh, my Eric!"

"Mrs. H, we need to get to the basement right away," said Neal. "Eric said Droon would fall in five days if we didn't act fast."

Eric's mother wiped her cheeks and stood. "Then I'm going with you."

"What?" said Neal. "Very funny, Mrs. H."

"It's not a joke. I'm going," the woman said. "He's my son. I'm his mother. I'm going."

"Yeah, but . . ." Neal murmured.

"I can help Eric," his mother said. "I'm certain of it."

When she saw the determination in Mrs. Hinkle's face, Julie realized they couldn't stop her from trying to help her son. She knew how she would feel if someone tried to stop *her* from helping her friend. Whatever Mrs. Hinkle was feeling must be ten times that. "Well, maybe just you can go —" she said.

The bedroom door opened, and in walked Mr. Hinkle. "Go? Go where?" he said. "Where are we going? Wait. Where's Eric? Eric —"

"Dear, there's no time to waste," said

Mrs. Hinkle. "Our son is a wizard. He's trying to keep the land of Droon free, but he's in trouble. Serious trouble."

As they explained everything, Mr. Hinkle's face went through a dozen expressions in rapid succession — disbelief, anger, concern, sorrow, and bewilderment.

Finally, he turned to the children.

"Eric is a wizard?" he asked.

"He is," said Julie.

"I wonder if he gets that from me," Mr. Hinkle said. "People say I'm kind of a wizard with the hedge clippers."

Julie smiled. Of course, it was really a blast from Keeah that had given Eric his powers, just as it was the wingwolf scratch that gave her her abilities. But it was just like Mr. Hinkle to find the funny in a terrible situation.

"Well, if Eric's in trouble, then we

are absolutely going to Dreen!" Mr. Hinkle said.

"First of all, it's *Droon*," said Neal. "And you really kind of have to do what we say. I mean . . . please?"

"Fair enough," said Mrs. Hinkle. "Let's go."

Moments later, they were crammed into the little closet under the basement stairs. They shut the door behind them, and Julie switched off the ceiling light.

Whoosh!

The floor beneath their feet vanished and became the top step of a staircase that curved through the air all the way to Droon.

"Amazing!" said Mr. Hinkle. "Who built these steps? They're very professional."

"Our friend the wizard Galen created them," said Julie, remembering her strange vision again. *He was so worried. I must tell him what I saw!*

Down and down they went, through swirling pink clouds, while Neal barked orders to the Hinkles every step of the way.

"Not too fast. Hold on to the railing. The stairs are slick. And be careful where it curves. The stairs have a mind of their own. Also, whatever you do, don't look down. Don't look up, either. You'll get dizzy."

"Neal, we've walked down stairs before," said Mr. Hinkle.

"Sorry. I guess I'm taking control again," Neal said. "It's the genie in me."

"You're a genie, Neal?" said Mrs. Hinkle. "Congratulations."

"Thanks. I really like my turban," he said.

Soon the children spotted a vast green plain sliced by several lines of blue water.

"Rivertangle," said Julie. "We've been here before. Be careful. Beasts are everywhere."

"One more thing," said Neal. "Sometimes the stairs vanish."

Mr. Hinkle smiled. "Now, that's pretty clever. The stairs vanish at the bottom so that the bad guys can't see them, right?"

Julie stole a look at Neal. "Not always. Sometimes they disappear at other times."

"What other times?" asked Mrs. Hinkle.

"Sometimes the stairs vanish *before* we get to the bottom," said Neal, picking up the pace.

Mrs. Hinkle paused. "Before? Like when?"

"Like now," said Neal as the steps quivered beneath their feet. "Like now. Now! NOW!"

All at once, the rainbow stairs wobbled and wiggled and faded into the air.

"You said to hold the railing," said Mr. Hinkle. "But there *is* no railing —"

And the two children and two parents plunged headfirst to the ground below.

Two

A Really Good Library

Luckily, the distance was not great, and their fall was broken by swift winds that swept upward just as they reached the ground. The little group tumbled harmlessly into the long soft grass of the river plains.

Unluckily, there was a band of hideous snakelike beasts camping nearby.

"Just our luck. Ugly snake guys!" whispered Neal, taking cover in the tall grass.

"Do you suppose they work for you-know-who?"

"Voldemort?" asked Mrs. Hinkle.

"No, Gethwing," said Julie, peering through the grass. She spotted the insignia of a crown on the beasts' packs. "The Crown of Wizards," she whispered. "They are part of Gethwing's army."

"Maybe we can reason with them," said Mrs. Hinkle.

"Beasts are creatures of few words," said Julie.

"Mostly one word," whispered Neal.

All at once, the big flat head of one of the snake creatures arched up and stared in their direction. "ATTACK!" it shrieked.

"That's the one!" said Neal.

As the snaky beasts leaped through the grass toward them, the kids rushed Mr. and Mrs. Hinkle to the nearest riverbank.

"Some beasts hate water," said Neal. "Let's hope —"

Alas, the scaly beasts did not hate water. No sooner had Neal and Julie dropped to the riverbank with the Hinkles than the snakes dived into the river.

"S-s-snakelings!" hissed one beast, darkening the clear water with its dirty scales.

"Yes-s-s, Slyvor!" said the others.

"Capture the old ones — they are slow!"

"Hold on. Who are you calling old?" said Mrs. Hinkle. "I haven't got one gray hair —"

"Neal, behind you!" cried Julie.

Neal turned too late. Two snakelings had wound their tails around the legs of Eric's parents and dragged them up the riverbank.

Before Neal could pop his turban on, three snakes swiped at him, sending him splashing into the water. "Help!"

Julie dived into the river to save him. As she dragged Neal to the far bank, she saw the snakelings tie the two Hinkle parents in thick ropes and hustle them back to their camp.

"Holy cow!" gasped Neal. "We lost Eric's parents! He's going to be so mad at us!"

"It was all my fault," said Julie. "I should have saved them first —"

"Shhh. Listen," said Neal.

"Harm them not," the snakeling leader was saying. "Tomorrow Gethwing comes-s-s. And I — Slyvor — shall get a prize for keeping them s-s-safe!"

"Get your paws off me!" Mr. Hinkle shouted. "This is my favorite jacket."

"You know, there are products to help that skin condition," said Mrs.

Hinkle. "You might feel better about yourself —"

"I feel so sorry for them," whispered Neal.

"Me, too," said Julie. "Captured the minute they set foot in Droon! Poor Hinkles."

"I mean the beasts," said Neal. "They'll wish they had never captured the Hinkles."

"I hope you're right," said Julie. "Their leader said they'll be safe. At least until Gethwing comes. We'll have to free them before then."

"Add it to the list," said Neal, edging away down the far riverbank. "We need to get the Moon Medallion and find a cure for Eric and stop the attack on Jaffa City and tell Galen your vision. Plus it might snow. Green snow!"

"It's going to be a busy day," said Julie.

Neal tugged his giant blue turban low on his brow. Then he grabbed Julie's hand, and they both jumped high in the air.

Whoooooosh!

Hand in hand, the friends soared westward away from Rivertangle, over the high green plains toward the Zorfendorf countryside. The sun had not yet risen over the horizon, but as they saw vast gray clouds massing in the distant east, they hoped Zorfendorf Castle was still free.

They flew mile after mile, over the deserted Dust Hills of Panjibarrh and farther south.

"We'd better hurry," said Neal. "We don't want a flock of wingwolves seeing us."

Julie hadn't been able to forget the scratch on her hand. It had tingled ever since the incident in the tree that morning.

"There's the castle," she said.

And there it stood. Zorfendorf's brilliant white stone turrets gleamed over the dark fields like a beacon.

"And there's Keeah —" said Neal.

The princess was racing across the tops of walls. "We've been waiting for you!" she shouted.

A few moments later, Julie and Neal landed inside the massive gate. Keeah ran to meet them.

"Snakelings surprised us at Rivertangle!" Neal told her. "Ugly, scaly dudes. They snapped up the Hinkles in, like, seconds."

Keeah shook her head. "Snakelings are nasty, but they're too afraid of Gethwing to cause any trouble. We'll rescue the Hinkles later. Come to the library. We have news."

"Me, too," said Julie as they hurried through the winding streets. "I had a vision I really have to tell Galen about."

The princess slowed at the castle steps.

"A vision?" she said. "Really?"

"I think it'll happen very soon," Julie said.

Keeah let out a deep breath. "I don't know how to say this, but . . . Galen is already gone."

Julie stopped. "What? But I had a vision of him just this morning. Anusa was guiding him. There was purple smoke —"

"Anusa led Galen away last night," said Keeah. "That wasn't the future you saw. It was the past."

Julie was stunned. "No . . ."

The princess took her hand. "I'm sorry. We have no time to waste. To the library."

They raced up the castle steps and down several hallways. They climbed a narrow winding staircase and ran down a wide straight one. They flashed through several corners and dived into a tunnel. Finally, they arrived at the massive library of the mysterious Prince Zorfendorf.

Hundreds of shelves lined the walls from floor to ceiling. Each was filled with thousands of books, overflowing stacks of paper, piles of maps, and bundles of scrolls.

And right there in the middle of them was their friend Max, swinging from shelf to shelf, muttering to himself, pulling out scrolls here, yanking out books there, and tossing them all over his shoulders in an avalanche of paper.

"Where is that ratty old book about ancient poisons?" he cried. "Or is it a scroll?"

Darting to and fro beneath Max, trying to catch whatever the spider troll threw down, was an implike creature that resembled a small wild dog.

His dark fur was spotted brightly from his snubby snout to this curly tail. He had very short rear legs, but his front paws were slender and delicate.

Julie recognized him at once. "It's Hob!"

"Hob is helping the search for Eric's cure," said the imp, tossing a pile of books and scrolls onto a big worktable.

Hob was the clever maker of magical masks the children had first met in the traveling city of Tortu. He always spoke of himself in the third person, as if he were someone else.

"A cure? Poisons?" said Neal. "Aren't we going to get the Moon Medallion?"

Keeah's face fell. "That's gone, too. My mother and father went to retrieve it from Jaffa City, but it had vanished."

"King Zello is assembling a team to search for it right now," said Hob. "In the meantime, we're finding another way to help Eric. With a cure!"

It was only then that Julie and Neal noticed another person in the library. They knew him, too. It was Thog, the giant caretaker of the castle's books. Normally as tall as a two-story house, Thog sat hunched in front of Galen's magic mirror. The scene on the mirror showed the old wizard stumbling along a dusty plain until the light faded and he couldn't be seen.

"When did this happen?" Julie asked.

"Last night, as the moon rose," said Thog.

So it's true, thought Julie. *I'm not predicting the future. I'm seeing the past. But why? How? What good is seeing what already happened?*

"Galen had been strange the past few days," said Keeah. "You remember when he told us of Anusa's coming. He knew he

would have to leave us. Every wizard has to."

Keeah was right. This wasn't the first time Galen had left them. Last time, he had gone willingly. When he returned, he was younger, stronger, refreshed, renewed.

This time seemed different. Julie remembered his face in her vision. Worried. Afraid of something. And what did he mean, "a hundred years"?

"Hold on! Is — this — it?" Max said, pulling an enormous scroll from the workbench. "Hob, quickly, the language!"

The spotted imp jumped to the scroll, scanned its tiny writing, then put one paw on his chin and the other on his head and began scratching with both. "Oh, dear, dear, dear!"

"What is it?" asked Keeah. "Tell us."

"The poison elixir," said Hob, "happens to be — are you ready? — fazool."

Max peered at the scroll. "Not . . . fazool?"

"Fazool?" said Thog, shaking his head.

"Fazool!" stated Hob.

"Okay, what is fazool?" asked Neal.

"Hush. Don't say that word!" said Hob.

"But you just said it —" started Neal.

"Never mind that!" Hob scolded. "Fazool is ancient. It is magical. It is rare. It is legendary! It is a green elixir that burns like fire. Worst of all, it is fatal. It kills whomever it touches. Instantly!"

"But Eric is not . . . you know," said Julie.

"Exactly!" said Hob. "Which means that a single drop of fazool must have been lost *before* Eric was poisoned."

"So we *can* cure Eric," said Keeah.

"Except," said Hob, "that the only cure *lies in that single drop*!"

"Then we'll find it," said Julie.

"Except that no one knows where it is!" said Hob.

"But if we don't find it, Eric will . . . you know," said Neal.

"Except . . ."

"Hob, please," said Keeah. "We have only five days, and this is the first one. Tell us, please."

The imp grumbled. "Very well. Hob will explain. If the elixir lost a drop, it must have happened between the Dark Lands, where it comes from, and the far north, where Eric was wounded."

"Poison traders!" said Max. He jumped onto the worktable, unrolled a large map, and traced his paws across it. "Their trade routes have crisscrossed the ancient Crimson Desert for centuries. . . ."

Max's paws came together. He gasped. "Koomba!"

"Koomba?" cried Hob. "The legendary

empire in the heart of the Crimson Desert? That is where we shall find our fazool!"

Koomba. At the mention of the word, Julie imagined vast cities shimmering with gold.

"Then let's go to Koomba," said Keeah. "We can't wait a second —"

"But Koomba is no more!" said the imp. "It was devoured by war and sandstorms ages ago. All that remains is an old trading post. This would mean nothing, except that the mysterious Sand Children are said to haunt the area."

Everyone waited for him to say more.

"And?" asked Keeah.

"The Sand Children and their leader, Empress Mashta," said Hob, "are mysterious and tiny, but they have one particular habit that could be just what saves Eric Hinkle!"

Everyone waited again.

"And that is?" asked Max.

"They steal!" cried Hob. "They say that in the darkness before each dawn, the Sand Children descend on desert travelers and steal bits and pieces of everything that isn't tied down. Where they take their bounty is unknown, but Hob knows first-hand about their thievery. Not long ago a pair of masks was stolen from him. If we find the Sand Children, we could very well find the missing drop of fazool — and Hob's masks!"

"A desert journey," said Neal. "Cool. Are we going to fly?"

Keeah shook her head. "Pilkas carry within them knowledge of the old trade routes. We'll ride them quickly but carefully and avoid any beastly encounters."

Julie nodded. *Beasts? Wingwolves!*

She ran her fingers over the tingling

scratch. It was pinker than before. She had definitely scratched it again in Eric's apple tree that morning.

"In the meantime," said Max, "Thog and I will construct a laboratory among these books. If you do find the drop of fazool, we shall quickly work to turn it into a cure!"

Keeah nodded. "The rest of us — to the Crimson Desert!"

Three

The Sandwiches There

"May luck and speed be with you!" called Max from the giant castle gate. "Dawn is but an hour away!"

The band of three children and one imp bade farewell from atop their team of heavily packed pilkas. They galloped due east, toward the rolling red dunes of the Crimson Desert.

No sooner had they left the green plains than the land turned scrubby and sandy.

"We have to be careful here," said Keeah. "Now that Sparr has joined Gethwing, his Ninns have returned to their evil ways. We may meet some today."

Lord Sparr was one of several "jewels" in Gethwing's Crown of Wizards. The others were Prince Ungast and Princess Neffu, Keeah's evil opposite. Although lately the Ninns had helped the kids, they had followed Sparr in joining Gethwing's war against Droon.

Once the little caravan passed the abandoned Dust Hills of Panjibarrh, they entered the vast and trackless sea of sand that fringed the Crimson Desert.

Sometimes they galloped along the crests of massive sand dunes. At other times, they hid quietly in the valleys between them while bands of roving beasts and swarms of wingwolves moved overheard.

"Soon, if we are lucky, we shall see the Sand Children," said Hob. "The little sprites are said to flit around like ghosts. Tales of their masterful thievery abound. They are . . . legendary!"

Neal laughed. "According to you, everything is legendary. Are *we* legendary?"

The imp giggled to himself. "Perhaps. Some of us. Only the future will tell."

The future.

That morning, Julie had had what she thought was a vision. But all she did was predict the past. How useful was that?

She rubbed the back of her hand, and the scratch tingled even more.

Neal laughed. "Hey, I just remembered something. Did you know that you can never go hungry in a desert?"

"Why not?" asked Keeah.

An image of Neal telling the same joke flashed through Julie's mind. She knew the answer to his riddle. "Because of the *sand which* is there. Right? The *sand-wiches* there?"

Hob chuckled. "Yes, quite!"

Neal grumbled. "I just heard that riddle yesterday, and you weren't even with me! How'd you know it already?"

Julie blinked. Neal was right. She *hadn't* been with Neal when he'd heard that joke. Was she having another vision of the past?

The pilkas rode to the crest of a tall dune, and the breeze changed direction. Warm and scented with a touch of burning wood, it moved over them, rustling their robes and scarves and jingling their tiny saddle bells ever so slightly.

"Well!" exclaimed Hob. "There may or may not be sandwiches, but there is certainly a lot of sand. And, if Hob is correct, it is red!"

The desert before them stretched on for miles and miles. Its dunes were massive and high and as red as the evening sun.

"The Crimson Desert!" whispered Keeah.

"The site of the legendary Koomba," said Hob. "Now lost forever!"

Lost or not, Julie couldn't help but picture the towering empire that once stood among the curious red dunes. In her mind, tall domes, fallen over time, resumed their upright shapes. Bridges rose out of the sand, linked to one another as far as the eye could see. Towers coiled themselves up, higher and higher, into the darkening sky.

"Nothing is left," said Keeah, "but a wasteland of sand."

No! thought Julie. *Is it just my mind playing tricks on me again? I see it all!*

But the instant she blinked, her image of old Koomba collapsed under waves of whirling sand, buried beneath centuries of desert, fading into nothing.

Only rolling red dunes remained.

Julie sighed. *Koomba was beautiful.*

"I see the trading post," said Neal. "Hurry."

The little band rode quickly to the foot of an enormous dune that winds had blown into the shape of a star. Just behind it stood a ramshackle little building made of planks from which all but the tiniest flecks of paint had been scoured away.

A battered sign hung on the outside.

KANTINA DU KOOMBA

A canvas canopy, worn ragged by the constant desert wind, hung low over a small front door that flapped on its squeaky hinges.

They heard gruff voices yelling from

inside, the clatter of thrown furniture, and the breaking of glass.

"Do you think poison traders are in there right now?" asked Neal.

"Perhaps," said Hob. "Whatever they trade, they are evil, no doubt. And that is why you shall thank Hob for being so clever. Some travelers pack food. Hob packs . . . masks!"

He dug his slender paws into the leather bags draped over his saddle and produced three masks. They were exquisitely detailed in bright blue, silver, and yellow.

"They will make you appear as beasts and traders," he said. "Since Gethwing's armies frequent this part of the world, you must blend in." He held out the masks.

"Where's your mask?" asked Keeah.

Hob smiled. "Hob is an imp. He doesn't have as much to overcome. Take one!"

Julie took the yellow mask and slipped it on. Moments later, she was tall, very tall, had four arms, a bulbous body, three tails, and a bumpy chin with three points on it.

Neal laughed. "Hey, good-looking!" He took the delicate silver mask and slipped it on. "Will this mask make me into a strong one?"

"Oh, you'll be strong," said Hob. "But you won't be *one*."

"What? No!" The moment the mask fell over his face, Neal's head grew outward and split into two. Then each nose grew straight out and ended in a fuzzy bush of white hair. "I hate my mask! I want the other one —"

"Mine!" said Keeah, snatching the blue mask.

As Keeah slipped it on, Hob grinned. "This mask gives you one tiny foot, five giant ears, and three noses. Or is it three ears, a tiny nose, and one giant foot?"

As it happened, Keeah had three feet, seven ears, and a flat nose the color of mustard. She was also covered with gray fur.

"Yours is so much better," Neal grumbled. "Why do I always get the mask that doesn't work right?"

"You do have an odd face," said Hob.

"I do not!" said Neal.

"Guys," said Keeah. "Time is wasting. Let's go in. And remember, we're beasts and we're traders. Be tough, okay? Let's go."

Taking one last moment to get into character, the four friends growled and grumbled and swaggered their way to the tavern door.

Four

At the Crossroads

A sudden gust of desert wind blew the children past the creaky door into the room, along with a wave of fine red sand.

"Shut the door!" growled a voice.

"Oh, sorry," said Julie.

"Don't be so polite," whispered Keeah.

Julie grunted in a beast voice. "I mean . . . shut your own door!"

When their eyes adjusted to the dim light of the room, the kids saw that it was filled with Ninns, the chubby red-faced warriors loyal to Lord Sparr. They were filthy after what appeared to be a long journey over the dunes.

"The Ninns are trading now?" whispered Neal.

"Hard times," said Hob.

A thing with a pudgy blue face, a rug of flat hair, and four eyes set very close together slammed a dented pot on the counter. He filled it with thick brown liquid until it foamed over the sides.

"Sit down and have some glunk!" he ordered.

"Mmm," said Neal. "Can I maybe have a glass?"

Every Ninn turned to him.

"A *dirty* glass!" Neal demanded.

"Hrumpf!" growled a loud voice.

The children turned and saw the large red face of a Ninn commander staring at them. In his pointy chin, fiercely arching eyebrows, and glaring eyes, they recognized a warrior who had helped them once upon a time.

"Captain Bludge?" whispered Keeah.

The Ninn narrowed his eyes suspiciously at the princess, who scratched her mustard-colored nose and shook her fur.

"I'm Thumpinius Bludge," he growled. "How do you know me?"

Julie thought fast. "We all know you, Captain Bludge. By reputation!" she said in as low a voice as she could muster. "You are known among the beasts as a fierce warrior. You are a friend to Gethwing and his dark forces."

The Ninn seemed to flinch at the mention of Gethwing's name. "Fierce, yes," he said. "But no longer captain. Gethwing has put his beasts in command now. We run errands for him. If only Sparr — the real Sparr — were back. But the dragon controls him now."

When Bludge mentioned the sorcerer, an image of Sparr flickered in Julie's mind. He was a little boy drawing pictures of birds. His small two-headed pet dog, Kem, was playing at his feet.

Stop it! she thought. *This isn't helping!*

"So, have you come to take the night-fox to Gethwing?" Bludge pulled with his hand, and a creature on an iron leash whimpered under his table.

It was a foxlike creature with jet-black fur and silver eyes. It was crouched, ready to pounce, but chains linked its feet together.

"Uh . . . no," said Neal. "We're just passing through."

"Have more glunk!" shouted the blue-faced thing at the counter.

Neal shrugged and filled up his dirty glass. "I pretend it's root beer."

Julie scanned the room. The Ninns muttered among themselves, their eyes downcast. She nudged Keeah. "They're not happy about doing stuff for Gethwing."

"Not at all," whispered the princess.

"So I guess we wait for the Sand Children to appear," whispered Neal. He kicked a chair out from under a table and plopped down into it, sipping his filthy glass of glunk.

A last glimmer of moonlight edged across the floor as the sky began to brighten. At that moment, the door flew open with a bang, and a giant furry foot entered the room.

It was followed by another, then a third, and finally by a wide, knobby body topped by a head like a lion's. It was furry all over except for the top, which was shiny.

"Ninns, your captain is here!" the creature grunted, blowing a foul breath into the room. "I — Captain Grunto — am the new ruler of the Ninns in the eastern province of the west country north of the southern border of the Crimson Desert. In other words — of you! Where is the nightfox? Our great leader, Gethwing, has commanded me to take the fox into the far north where . . . no one . . . shall ever . . . see him . . . again!"

Bludge stood up. "Why? What has the fox done?"

"Never you mind!" grunted the beast leader, the bald spot on his head turning beet red. "Just give me the fox!"

But the moment Bludge tugged the little creature out from under the table, something streaked across the room. A chair next to Bludge toppled to the floor. Then came a clatter of chains. Suddenly — *whoosh!* — the nightfox was gone, and Bludge was left holding an empty leash!

"Arrgh!" growled Captain Grunto. "Where's the fox?"

"The Sand Children!" whispered Julie. "Guys, it must be —"

"Hey!" Neal swung around as a tiny figure leaped away from him. Neal's giant blue turban was in its hands. "Give that back!"

In a flash, the tavern was alive with little shapes dancing and diving from table to floor to ceiling to door and back again.

"My boot!" shouted a Ninn.

"My nose ring!" yelled a second.

"My glunk!" cried the lion-headed beast.

"Yoo-hoo, children!" whispered a voice. "Time to vanish!"

Julie whirled around and saw a tiny red and silver figure holding the tavern window open. A band of silvery shapes leaped out the window, their little arms laden with treasure.

"Help me catch one!" said Julie.

"But how?" asked Neal. "They're so fast!"

"I'll nab one!" Keeah leaped past a table at a tiny shape flying across the room. Chuckling, the thing flattened itself and slid over a tabletop, then jumped onto the windowsill and out across the sand.

Keeah reached for it, slipped, and stumbled over a chair. "Big, dumb three feet!" She hit the floor, and her mask tumbled

beneath Bludge's table. In an instant —
pling! — she was herself again.

Everyone stared at Keeah.

"Um . . . hi?" she said.

"A child!" Grunto boomed. "A girl child!
A princess girl child! A princess girl child of
Droon! Princess Keeah of Droon! Ninns, as
your captain, I demand you capture her!"

"Capture *us*, you mean," said Neal,
whipping off his mask, turning back into
himself, and jumping next to Keeah. "Well,
I mean, not *capture* us. We're the good
guys, after all, and we stick together —"

"Neal, hush," said Julie. She, too,
removed her mask and stood with Keeah.

"There are three and a half of us now,"
said Hob, scampering behind the children.

"Then, Ninns — do that!" shouted the
beast leader. "Capture them! Capture all
of them!"

"No, you don't!" cried Julie. "Everyone to the star dune!"

"Except you bad guys," said Neal. "Not you. But us. The good guys —"

"Neal, hush!" cried Keeah as the children burst from the tavern and charged up the great star-shaped dune, with thirty-five angry Ninns on their tail!

* Five *

Below the Sand

"I saw the Sand Children run here," said Julie, leading the way up the tall dune. She reached the top just in time to see a flash of red and silver disappear into the sand.

"What?" said Keeah. "Where did they —"

"There," said Julie, pointing.

At the very tip, where the crests of five individual dunes met, was a narrow opening in the sand. It was perfectly round and was bordered by a band of silver.

"The entrance," she said.

"But the entrance to what?" asked Neal.

"To safety," said Hob, looking nervously behind him. "Unless you want the Ninns to get you! Bludge is coming, he is yelling, and Hob saves himself!"

The imp shoved past the others and dropped right into the opening.

"Capture them!" yelled Bludge, who was already halfway up the dune.

"I miss Hob," said Neal. "Me next!" He, too, disappeared through the opening.

Julie and Keeah looked at each other, then quickly followed Neal and Hob. A moment later, they found themselves at the top of a wooden staircase that teetered and wobbled crazily from just under the surface to the distant ground below.

"It's hollow!" said Keeah. "The entire dune is hollow!"

"And Bludge wants to see it, too!" said Neal as the former Ninn leader jumped into the entrance hole above them. Luckily, he was too large to fit and got stuck.

"Arrgh!" he yelled. "Ninns, get me free!"

"Quickly, down the stairs," said Hob.

As the friends clambered down, they couldn't help noticing that the rickety steps were made of planks of weathered wood.

"The Sand Children must have built the stairs from pieces of the tavern," said Keeah.

Although hundreds of feet from ceiling to floor, the space under the dune was large and open like a cavern. An intricate pattern of planks crisscrossed the ceiling to keep the sand in place. Odd structures dotted the space below all the way into the shadowy distance. The kids guessed that they were houses. They were made of more wooden slats tied together with cloths and rope. They ranged along streets of red sand, lit by flames reflected in mirrors and plates and goblets, giving the whole sandy cavern a silvery glow.

Among the houses were Ninn war belts fashioned into hammocks, ancient armor hammered and flattened into bridges, and here and there wagon wheels made into merry-go-rounds.

Lamps fashioned of dented glunk pots hung from posts and lit the way down sandy paths that curved off into the darkness.

"This is kind of amazing," said Neal when they reached the bottom of the stairs.

"And kind of beautiful," said Keeah.

"And very legendary!" said Hob.

"Indeed it is!" said a high, strange voice.

The four friends turned and saw a short, stout woman dressed in red and silver robes. A crown of silver cloth circled her brow, under which long silver hair cascaded nearly to her waist.

"Greetings and welcome to Koomba," the little woman said. "I am Mashta, Empress of the Sand Children."

"I am Princess Keeah," said Keeah.

The two rulers bowed to each other.

"We are ghostly little folk," said Mashta, waving her arms at the surrounding streets, "who arise just before dawn from the red dunes on the fringes of the Dark Lands. Children, come and greet our visitors!"

The streets came alive with little shapes.

The Sand Children were no larger than a foot tall and were dressed in silver tunics and slippers. Their faces were eager and childlike as they huddled around their empress, who stood taller than they by only an inch or two.

The little folks' arms were still full of the treasures they'd stolen at the tavern. Freed from its chains, the black-furred nightfox scampered along with them.

"Is this the empire of Koomba?" asked Julie.

"Yes . . . and no," said Mashta, flinging her robes behind her to reveal a short staff hanging at her waist. "All that remains of the original Koomba are the pathways and roads, shells of buildings, and passages into the dark. But when the beasts drove us underground, we decided to create our own empire in the underdune, using what we find and borrow and . . . take. This is our Koomba now."

"The underdune," said Keeah. "A beautiful word —"

"Arr-arr-arrgh!"

Pop!

Bludge was finally yanked up and out of the entrance hole above them. The Sand Children giggled brightly.

"Ho-ho-ho!" said Mashta, her whole body shaking. "We are sometimes sad, but not for long. We have too much beauty and wonder around us! The underdune is our living museum of trinkets and treasures."

Julie glanced at Neal and Keeah. Did the Sand Children have a drop of fazool among their treasures?

The empress motioned the friends into a small house. A pedestal lit by candles stood at the center of a simple room. On the pedestal sat a small tasseled pillow.

"What's this?" asked Neal. "A sleeping lumpy?"

Mashta laughed. "No. Look closely and you will see the only known claw of a young wingwolf."

"A wingwolf?" Julie rubbed her hand again and fixed her eyes on a small object as white as a bone and as sharp as a blade.

"Now, *that* is legendary!" said Hob, his face aglow in the candlelight.

"Exactly," said Mashta. "Young wingwolves shed their claws like we lose baby teeth. The legend is that at birth, wingwolves are able to fly and change shape, but they also have a third power."

"What power?" asked Julie.

"Alas, once young wingwolves lose their claws, they are said to forget what their third power is," the empress said.

"And so legends are born," said Hob.

Julie remembered the exact moment she was first scratched by the flying wolf. At first it stung; then she had felt a tingling sensation up her arms and neck and the unmistakable feeling of being special.

She loved to fly. And changing shape was amazingly useful. And yet, she always felt she could do more.

Could she have a *third* power?

"But something tells me you are here for another reason," Empress Mashta said.

Keeah drew in a breath. "We're looking for a poison that has cursed our friend," she said.

"A cursed poison?" said Mashta. "You mean the dreaded . . . fazool."

As soon as the empress mentioned the word, the Sand Children whispered among themselves and drew closer to her.

"They fear fazool," she said. "But mostly the hideous monster that protects it."

"Monster?" asked Neal. "Nobody mentioned a monster."

"A terrifying creature," said the empress. "We never should have taken the silver vial from the tavern, but, alas, it was so shiny. And cool to the touch. Little did we know what poison burned within. Soon the vial vanished, and just as soon an unspeakable monster began to haunt the dark passages beyond our little underground village. We have never ventured into the Forbidden Passages."

Keeah looked toward the shadowy corners of the cavern. "Monster or not, if the fazool still exists, we have to find it. Time is running out for our friend. And for Droon."

"You must love your friend a great deal to risk such danger," said Mashta. "We cannot lead you into the Forbidden Passages, but if you must go, you may take the machine —"

"Machine?" said Neal. "What kind of machine?"

"Better to see it than to hear about it. Follow me."

Mashta led the four friends down one path after another until they came to a large shape covered by a red cloth. Tugging the cloth, the empress revealed what looked like an elephant with a blue hide, enormous twin trunks, and great batwing-shaped ears. It was made of iron plates and rivets and pistons and rods.

"A tuskadon?" said Keeah.

"An iron tuskadon," said Mashta. "It was here when the Sand Children and I arrived. None of us knows how it came to be here."

The tuskadon's front left foot was frozen in the air, raised high as if ready to take a step.

"Holy cow, this is so cool!" said Neal,

running his hands over the iron plates that formed the machine's hide.

All at once, there came a howl. The nightfox yelped excitedly when it saw the machine. The little animal leaped so high, it landed on the machine's giant head, right next to the control cabin.

"Hob thinks we have a passenger," said Hob.

The nightfox pawed one of the machine's ears — *pop!* — a hatch opened, and the creature slid inside. The next moment — *Foom! Thunk! Plooof!* — steam rose from the machine's giant trunk.

"I think we have a driver!" said Keeah.

The kids climbed up the riveted hide of the tuskadon and squeezed themselves through the hatch into the cabin. As the motors churned and chugged, the tuskadon coughed and sneezed alarmingly, as it if would explode from the pressure.

"Open the snouts —" said Neal.

"You mean the trunks?" said Julie.

"Whatever!"

Seeing a big lever, Hob took it and pushed forward with all his might. A blast of steam burst from the tuskadon's massive trunks, blowing sand everywhere, and the giant machine took a step — *phoom!* The ground shook beneath it. It took another step — *phoom!* And another and another.

The creature was walking!

"Into the Forbidden Passages!" said Hob.

"To find the elixir!" added Keeah.

Six

About a Boy

No sooner had the kids entered the Forbidden Passages than fierce winds roared about, pelting the tuskadon's iron hide with sand as hard as frozen rain.

"Nasty weather in here," said Neal.

"I wonder if the passages lead somewhere," said Julie. "Maybe out to the surface again?"

Gears groaned and spun and clacked.

The tuskadon thundered down the paths as fast as its iron legs could take it.

"I hope it knows where to go," said Keeah.

In fact, the machine seemed to want to go off the paths. The great iron tuskadon lurched constantly to the left, and sparks flew like fireworks as it scraped the sides of the tunnel.

The nightfox growled once — "Rrrr!" — then swatted a paw across the control panel. The machine righted itself, turned, and powered directly off into a side tunnel.

"Hmm," said Hob. "Almost as if that was no accident —"

"Everyone," said Keeah, "look up here."

Julie's heart hammered in her chest when she saw the crude drawings of birds scratched across the ceiling of the cabin.

She recalled her earlier image of little Sparr drawing pictures of birds. And here they were!

"I think Sparr made those pictures!" she said.

The nightfox grumbled softly and hopped up next to Julie, looking out the porthole.

"Are you serious?" said Neal. "Sparr?"

"When he was young," said Julie. "Don't ask me how I know, but I think . . . this machine was a sort of toy for him —"

"Hob, slow down," said Keeah. "There's something blocking the passage."

The tunnel ahead had caved in. Giant chunks of rock and dense mounds of sand were piled from floor to ceiling and wall to wall across the passage.

"Hob, please stop," said Keeah.

"Hob can't stop!" cried the imp. He yanked back on the lever, but the tuskadon kept pressing forward. It slammed into one block and pushed it aside. It struck another. "It wants to keep going! It's out of control!"

The machine struck the tumbled stone and kept stepping forward like a toy with batteries that hits a wall over and over. The gears ground, the mechanical legs squealed, and the steam built up until the iron animal shook and quaked.

"It's going to explode!" cried Hob. "Everyone out!"

The four friends and the nightfox jumped from the tuskadon just as its trunks blasted an enormous cloud of steam. The sand in the tunnel blew up into a storm that showered over the kids.

When the dust finally cleared, the tus-kadon stood tilted and motionless. It had wedged itself firmly into the tunnel.

"Terrific," said Neal. "Stuck in the Forbidden Passages with no ride."

Coughing and gasping for air, Hob said, "That toy . . . is *not a toy*!"

"Look," said Keeah.

The explosion had dislodged one of the giant blocks obstructing the passage, creating a slender gap in the rubble.

Julie peered into the gap. She saw a glimmer of light in the far distance.

"What can you see —" said Neal.

"Shhh," she said, holding her hand up.

Everyone fell quiet. Closing her eyes and concentrating, Julie heard the sound of something hissing from somewhere beyond the collapsed wall.

"Uh-oh." Julie backed away.

The hissing grew louder.

"Is that what Hob thinks it is?" asked Hob.

Neal gulped. "If you're thinking what I think you're thinking, then I think so!"

A tentacle, green and thin and dappled with shiny scales, slithered out through the collapsed stone and felt around in the light. A row of tiny teeth clacked on the end of the tentacle.

Hob jumped. "The legendary monster!"

"Maybe I should blast it right now," said Keeah, her fingers already beginning to spark.

A second tentacle emerged from the hole, enlarging it, and Julie could see more of the glimmering light beyond it.

"I have an idea," she said. "If we draw the monster out here, one of us can sneak through the hole to the other side. That's probably where the fazool is."

"Draw it out here? Where we are?" said Neal. "Uh-huh, and what's Plan B?"

"Julie's right," said Keeah as a third tentacle pushed its way past the others,

enlarging the hole even further. "Maybe we can keep it busy long enough for someone to find the fazool."

Soon a fourth, fifth, and sixth tentacle emerged from the hole, pulling through a body as long as a squid but covered with scales. The fangs at the tip of each tentacle chomped constantly.

Julie could think of nothing but the light beyond the cave-in. "I'll go," she said. "I want to. I have to."

Her friends looked at her.

"All right, then," said Keeah. "We'll cover you. Neal?"

"I'm on it." He tugged his turban low on his brow, twisted his fingers, and — *plink!* — he suddenly wielded a gnarly club in his hands.

"Rooo!" went the nightfox.

"I know. I look good, don't I?" said Neal.

"Wish me luck," said Julie.

"We'll need some, too," said Keeah.

Julie went deep into herself to a place of calm and quiet. The outside world seemed to fade away, and all that remained were her own thoughts.

So.

I've got to get past the monster.

Then what?

We'll see.

Two tentacles flipped wildly, snapping at Keeah. She blasted them, and Neal jumped forward, swinging his club.

"Now!" cried Hob. "Julie, go —"

Julie ducked, dodged to the side, and ran forward, leaping through the hole and out the other side.

Just as she had seen when she had peered in, the path inside was gold. Not gold from light or reflected sand, but genuine gold, beaten to a flat surface.

Turning, she saw Neal and Keeah fighting the monster, while Hob and the nightfox huddled behind the stalled tuskadon.

"Good luck," she whispered.

Then she ran toward the glittering path ahead.

Seven

The Face of Fazool!

Soon the noises of battle faded completely, and all Julie could hear were her own soft footsteps tapping along the golden path.

"This is so beautiful," she said to herself. "And so strange. Is this a street of ancient Koomba? Is that where I am?"

All at once, the street turned, and the passage's low ceiling gave way to a high, ornate vault, also made of shimmering gold.

On either side of her stood the remains of once-great buildings toppled upon themselves. Huge blocks of silvery stone, fallen towers etched in brass, and the remains of turreted walls surrounded her. Great hanging lamps of gold and crystal and the shreds of banners torn and ragged all swung in sudden breezes, and the air sang with the plinking of tiny bells.

"Koomba does exist," Julie said to herself. "And I've found it!"

Rubbing her hand, she realized that the wingwolf scratch was becoming inflamed.

A warm desert breeze touched her cheek.

Looking beyond the buildings and into the distance, she saw what could only be the brightening light of day.

"The passages lead out," she whispered.

As she approached the light, however, she glimpsed a curving passage of fallen blocks to her left. It was barely lit by its own light, but seemed to her as bright as a beacon.

"That way then," she whispered.

Drawn by the light, Julie rushed forward, trusting her instincts.

Her instincts let her down.

She tripped twice over uprooted paving stones, bumped her shoulders on tilted lampposts, banged her knees over and over on stone blocks, and barely escaped knocking herself out.

Then she stopped. A smoky purple cloud seemed to float up from nothing and fill the passage.

"What? Oh, not now, please," she said. "Not the past —"

But the cloud would not stop. It grew and grew like smoke from a bottle, and there was Galen, standing near her, his face just as it had been before, worried and afraid.

"Galen?" she said. "What is it?"

He answered in a faraway voice, as if he spoke from somewhere distant. He did not look directly at Julie.

"By the time you see me here — whoever you are — I shall be gone. Even a wizard cannot choose the moment of going. But listen close! Fearing for the safety of Jaffa City, I have stolen and hidden its most precious artifact, the Moon Medallion —"

"*You* stole it!" said Julie.

But the wizard continued. "To keep it safe . . . none shall lay eyes upon it . . . for a hundred years!"

"But we need it! Eric asked for it —"

As before, a second shape and voice appeared from the swirling smoke. "Wizard, come. . . ." And both figures vanished into thin air.

When the vision cleared, Julie looked down where Galen had stood. There, so tiny she might have missed it, lay a small silver vial.

"The fazool!"

But when Julie bent to reach for it, the vial's top came loose, and a single drop of green liquid seeped out. It hissed where it struck the floor. Right before her eyes, the drop transformed itself into the monster with fiery scales and snapping tentacles.

Julie blinked. When she opened her eyes again, she saw only the empty vial on the floor.

The image repeated time and again in her mind with the sound of bells chiming, until finally she understood what it meant.

"That's what happened!" she cried. "It's not a vision of the future. It's a vision of the past! Just like my vision of Galen in the violet fog!"

And Julie realized that there was nothing to find in the passages but the fallen remains of an ancient empire. She and her friends had already discovered the elixir.

Three hundred paces behind her, Neal, Keeah, Hob, and the nightfox were battling it right now!

The elixir was the monster.

The monster was the elixir!

She laughed aloud. "Seeing into the past is an amazing power! It *is* helpful! It's important. It can help save Droon!"

When Julie picked up the vial, she found it frosty cold to the touch. Holding it tightly, she sprinted back through the dark passages. This time she knew every turn to make.

Crawling out beyond the collapsed wall, Julie found her friends deep in battle with the monster.

"Don't hurt it!" she cried.

"But it's hurting us!" shouted Neal. "It's burning me — ouch!" He swatted the beast's coiling tentacles, but they were too swift and too many for him. Grabbing him by the legs, the monster hoisted him off the floor and dropped him with a thud. Neal's shirt smoked as he staggered to his feet. "See what I mean?"

"Julie, stand back!" said Keeah, aiming her fingers to blast the monster.

"Wait!" cried Julie. "Don't shoot! The monster *is* the elixir. I saw it in the passage. The vial is cold, but the heat of the air made it grow. We need a spell to turn it cold again —"

All at once, Neal jumped up. "Snow!" he said. "This is what my dream was all about. I can do this. Genies are great at making snow —"

"Please do it quickly!" said Hob.

As Keeah sprayed sparks here and there and the nightfox barked at the monster, Neal uncoiled his miniature scroll of instructions and recited an ancient charm. In moments, the first tiny snowflakes, as green as spring grass, began to fall in the passage.

As the flakes fell, the monster stopped its attack. It raised its tentacles to the falling snow as if to capture each flake. And it grew smaller and smaller by the instant.

Soon all that remained was a single drop of green liquid, which Julie urged into the empty vial. She snapped on the lid and locked it. The fazool was theirs!

"Safe and sound," Julie said.

"That was amazing," said Keeah. "How did you know that?"

Julie smiled. "It's as simple as remembering stuff I never knew! Guess what else. The ruins of Koomba lie beyond that cave-in. I saw a vision of Galen there, only this time, I heard every word. He stole the Moon Medallion and hid it away — for a hundred years, he said."

Hob murmured to himself. "A riddle, no doubt. Hob shall put his devious mind to work on it immediately!"

"Another thing I discovered in the passage is that the roads lead out to the surface of the sand. We can escape —"

At that moment, they heard yells echoing down the passages to them. "Heeelllp!"

"We can escape to the surface," said Hob. "But Mashta needs our help!"

"Then that's where we're going," said Keeah. "Stand back." She blasted the rocks around the tuskadon, freeing it.

Climbing inside, the five friends

powered it up, turned it around, and thundered back down the passages to the cavern and Mashta and her people.

When they arrived, the sand folk were huddled at the bottom of the wobbly stairs, right under the entrance hole.

"It's terrible!" said Mashta. "That horrible Captain Grunto has called more beasts than I have ever seen! They will destroy our little Koomba!"

"Your *big* Koomba," said Julie. "The lost empire still exists! I found it beyond the Forbidden Passages —"

Suddenly, a great roar came from the surface. It was only when the friends climbed the stairs to the opening and peeked out that they heard one particular voice.

"You don't have to be so rude," it said. "Even if you *are* a giant snake."

"S-s-silence, old ones-s-s!"

"Please don't speak that way to my wife," said another voice. "And for the last time, take your paws off my jacket!"

The children turned to one another.

"The Hinkles?" whispered Keeah. "At the trading post? That means the snakelings are here, too!"

"Snakelings? Here?" said Hob. "My goodness. They are legendary!"

Eight

Krazy Kantina!

"Legendary, my foot," said Neal as the kids stood at the crest of the star dune. "Snakelings are plain old nasty!"

A column of the snakelike beasts assembled in front of the trading post, while the lion-headed Captain Grunto and Slyvor the snakeling leader dragged Mr. and Mrs. Hinkle inside.

Even from that distance, the kids could hear Eric's parents complaining.

"I don't think the Hinkles really under-stand the danger they're in," said Julie.

"People, we need to get down there," said Keeah. "We have to get them free."

"And we shall help," said Mashta. The Sand Children murmured agreement.

Keeah thanked the empress. "It could get very dangerous. I wouldn't want you and your children to be hurt. You can always use the passages Julie found to escape to the desert beyond."

"We will not run," said Mashta, "but wait for your signal to help, if you need us."

"Good," said the princess. "Julie, Neal, Hob, come on."

Julie secured the vial of fazool in her belt, and she, Neal, Hob, and the nightfox followed Keeah down the dune. Keeping out of sight of the horde of snakelings, they circled around the back of the trading post and peeked through the broken planks.

"We could cause a distraction," whispered Hob. "More genie snow, perhaps?"

"There are far too many of them," said Keeah. "Even with some good bad weather."

"How about that one word that we don't like so much?" asked Neal.

Julie smiled. "You mean 'attack'?"

"That's the one," said Neal.

The children looked at one another. They all nodded in agreement.

"One . . . two . . . three . . . attack!" said Keeah.

The five friends burst into the tavern just as the snakelings chained Mr. and Mrs. Hinkle into chairs. The slithering creatures hissed and growled when they saw the kids.

"Let Eric's parents go!" said Keeah, her fingers sizzling with violet sparks. "Or fear the wrath of Keeah!"

"And the wrath of Julie!"

"And the wrath of Neal!" said Neal.

"And Hob," said Hob.

"Halt!" Slyvor slid forward, grinning. "You children don't want to ris-s-sk a battle. These Upper Worlders-s-s could get hurt. Wait. Did I s-s-say hurt? I meant . . . *very* hurt!"

Captain Grunto growled. "So give us the fazool *and* the nightfox."

"And you can have the old ones-s-s," added Slyvor.

"I still don't like it when you call us old," said Mrs. Hinkle. "Ever hear of being polite?"

"Ever hear of being *s-s-silent*?" hissed the snake leader.

"Let's think about that," said Neal. "Mmm . . . no. Wait. Did I say no? I meant *very* no."

Captain Grunto grunted. "Lord Gethwing comes soon. He will be angry if you don't do what we say. First give me the fox."

The nightfox growled. "Rrrr . . ."

"And if we won't?" asked Julie.

"Yeah, if we won't?" said Neal.

"Then we overpower you all," said Grunto. "Ninns, surround them!"

"Yes . . . *Captain*," Bludge grumbled. He signaled his entire troop of red warriors to surround the children.

"What do you say we talk about this?" said Mr. Hinkle. "One or two friendly words might help sort this out —"

"No words!" said Grunto. "Time for words is over. I prefer numbers. . . ."

"Numbers?" said Neal scornfully. "Can you even count?"

"What kind of numbers?" asked Keeah.

"Numbers like . . . ten!" said Grunto. "And . . . nine!"

"Oh, those numbers," said Mrs. Hinkle.

"Eight!" said the beast.

"I bet I know where this is heading," said Neal.

Bludge unslung his war club and began swinging it in the air.

"Seven!" boomed Grunto.

Neal nodded. "Yep, I know what's coming!"

"Six! Four!"

"No fair, you skipped five!" said Neal.

"Three . . . two . . . one!"

Nine

The Great Mask Mystery

No one moved.

"Wait for it," said Slyvor. He breathed in, then squealed his favorite word.

"ATTACK!"

Before the Ninns could move, there came a sound from the dunes outside.

"Laaaa!"

"What's-s-s that?" demanded the snakeling.

That was Empress Mashta.

At the sound of her war cry, Sand Children flooded into the tavern from every direction. There were hundreds of them. The tiny silvery folk leaped on the Ninns, they dived at the snakelings, they nipped, they pinched, they poked at Captain Grunto.

"Oww!" cried Bludge, swatting the air with his club, but managing only to hit his own foot.

Mashta urged her people on. "Steal their weapons! Untie their bootlaces! Flick their noses! Pinch their ears!"

The snakelings shrieked. The Ninns howled. The lion-headed beast bellowed.

"Cool!" said Mr. Hinkle. "A real Droon battle!"

"Which we'll survive only if you follow me," said Keeah. "We have the elixir to cure Eric."

"Yes!" cheered Mrs. Hinkle. "Let's go!"

With a quick blast, Keeah broke the chains binding Eric's parents. "Come on!"

Together with Julie, Neal, Hob, and the nightfox, she hurried the Hinkles away from the snakes. While the chaos of battle continued all around them, they crawled out of the tavern and slunk along the back of the building straight to the pilkas.

Seeing the children leave, Bludge knocked his way out of the building.

"This time you'll not escape!" he boomed.

"Princess, hide in the underdune and escape through the passages!" shouted Mashta. "We'll cover you all! Hurry!"

"The underdune," said Mr. Hinkle. "I'm not sure —"

"Honey," said Mrs. Hinkle, "do what the little woman says."

The four friends, the nightfox, and Eric's parents charged to the crest of the dune.

"Wow, a drain," said Mr. Hinkle. "Is that why they call this the world of Drain?"

"It's *Droon*," said Neal. "And hurry up down there. Please?"

Seconds later, they were racing down the stairs into the underdune.

Taking his club in both hands, Bludge battered the opening to the dune above them.

Sand fell away until the hole was large enough, and he jumped in. His band of Ninns followed him.

"Into the passages. And freedom!" said Julie.

"That sounds good," said Mrs. Hinkle.

"Not so fast!" shouted Bludge. Bouncing once, twice, he skidded to the bottom of the stairs, then leaped through the air and slid headfirst down the sandy street. With his massive arms spread wide, he caught the nightfox and Neal.

"Aha!" Bludge yelled. "Captured!"

The three of them slid across the ground, blowing wave after wave of sand over themselves.

Neal sneezed once, twice, and that was it. When the nightfox sneezed, however, something else happened.

Plunk! Plunk! Two masks the color of night fell to the sandy ground. Everyone froze.

Hob jumped up. "Hob's legendary masks!" he shouted. "The nightfox was wearing them. Hob has found his masks at last!"

But where the nightfox had been, another creature took shape. What stood there was no longer a small, pointy-snouted, long-eared nightfox but a large gray dog with two wide-eyed faces on two furry heads.

Two heads the children had seen before.

"Kem?" gasped Julie.

"Roo-rooo!" barked the creature's twin heads.

It *was* Kem, Lord Sparr's pet dog, whom the children had not seen in a very long time.

"*That's* why he recognized Sparr's tus-kadon!" said Keeah.

The Ninn warriors stopped short. Bludge lowered his giant club. There was a moment of silence as Kem's large brown eyes met his own.

Then Bludge spoke. "Gethwing wants to hide Kem in the far north?"

"Hide such a cute guy?" said Mr. Hinkle, stooping to scruff Kem's four ears.

Bludge nodded. "But why?"

Julie knew the answer. She had seen it in her vision. "Gethwing wants to hide him from Lord Sparr. Because if Sparr saw Kem, he might remember his good side and turn against Gethwing!"

"Just like Eric did when he saw the photograph I gave you," said Mrs. Hinkle.

Bludge sniffled. He blew his nose. "It's good to have Lord Sparr's doggie back. If Kem is free, Sparr can return to the way he was . . . and to us —"

Right then, they heard thumping on the sand above.

"Bludge!" called Grunto from outside the dune. "Bring the nightfox! And the elixir! And the children!"

"And the old ones-s-s, too!" added Slyvor.

"Okay, we've had just about enough of that!" said Mrs. Hinkle.

"Ninns have had enough of Grunto and Slyvor, too!" said Bludge.

"S-s-surrender," continued Slyvor, "or

we attack you all, and nothing below the s-s-sand will s-s-survive!"

As if to prove his point, the army of snaky beasts slithered around and around the dune entrance, until sand from the ceiling began to sift down through the air.

"Ninns!" boomed Grunto. "You are traitors to the great moon dragon! You will suffer with the others! Ten . . . nine . . ."

"We have just recovered the ancient empire of Koomba. Is it to be buried all over again?" said Mashta.

"And is Hob to be crushed?" whimpered Hob.

". . . three . . . one!"

The snakelings growled and hissed and gnashed their fangs, waiting for the signal.

Then it came.

"ATTACK!"

"I really don't like that word," sighed Neal.

Ten

The Way Up and Out

The ceiling of the giant cavern quaked, and sand showered everyone like rain.

"Children, escape to the passages and into the desert," said Mashta. "We shall look for a new home."

"No," said Bludge. "Ninns will defend the Sand Children. And the humans. And Koomba! We will do this for the Lord Sparr we once knew!"

"Rooo!" howled Kem. Then he ran for the tuskadon and leaped into its cabin.

"Wait a second. Sparr's toy," said Julie. "Of course! Everyone, come on. We can defeat the beasts, and we can do it right here!"

It was decided in an instant. Bludge would lead his red-faced warriors and the Sand Children through the passages and up to the surface, while the kids would defend the underdune.

Neal, Julie, Keeah, the Hinkles, and Hob crowded inside the iron beast with Kem. They revved up the machine's giant engine. It quivered and wobbled. It shook and teetered. They drove it right under the star dune's entrance hole.

"Here we come!" announced Slyvor. And the snakelings slid into the entrance and slithered down the stairs.

"Trunks . . . up?" asked Julie.

"Trunks . . . up!" Keeah affirmed.

The steam built up more and more until the iron beast seemed ready to explode.

"Now?" said Neal.

"No," said Keeah.

Sand fell on the trembling tuskadon, and the snakelings came closer.

"Now?" asked Julie.

"Not yet," said Keeah.

The tuskadon rocked on its iron legs. The plates on its sides rattled and shook. The rivets began to loosen one by one.

"Now?" cried Hob.

"Now!" said Keeah.

Together, the children pulled the lever.

WHOOOOOM!

A gigantic spout of steam burst from the tuskadon's iron trunks. It shot upward, blowing the top of the dune completely off. Sand exploded everywhere, and the shrieking, hissing beasts were thrown back into the Crimson Desert.

When Slyvor stopped rolling, he was twisted in a knot and struggled to stand. "Where are the little ones-s-s and the elixir?"

At that moment, Bludge and his Ninns clambered out of the distant passages back up to the surface.

Using all the slyness he could muster, the Ninn leader shouted, "Look there! I see them escaping! Far away across the dunes. The children, the elixir, and the nightfox! Hurry, beasts! Let's go after them!"

"Follow!" squealed Slyvor.

"Follow!" boomed Captain Grunto.

While Bludge and four other Ninns hid, the rest of their red-faced compatriots drew the beasts quickly across the red sand and into the far distance.

Leaving the tuskadon on the floor of the underdune, Julie, Keeah, Neal, Hob, the Hinkles, Kem, Bludge, and four Ninns met Mashta and her tiny people. They stood alone under the brightening skies.

"Those are good Ninns," Bludge said of his fellow warriors. "Good men. Loyal and true. After such a long while, I am happy to be myself again."

"Good for you," said Empress Mashta. "And thank you for your help. We desert folk will inhabit the ancient empire of Koomba, lost no longer."

The Sand Children cheered.

"With Kem's help," said the red-faced warrior, "our little band of five Ninns will reunite Lord Sparr with his long-lost past. We will turn him away from Gethwing's power and break the Crown of Wizards forever!"

"Hooray for Bludge!" shouted the Ninns. "Our captain once more!"

Bludge bowed his head, then raised it. "Our first mission — to find Lord Sparr!"

"Rooo-rooo!" wailed Kem excitedly.

With that as their signal, Captain Bludge and his band raced across the sands with Kem at the lead, plotting Lord Sparr's return.

Julie gave the silver vial to Keeah with a smile. "Hard to believe, but I guess we did it."

"Ah, that reminds me," said Empress Mashta. "Ahem . . ."

A Sand Child stepped forward, holding the velvet pillow they had seen before. On the pillow sat the young wing-wolf's claw.

"Julie, please accept this as our gift," said the empress. "As a remembrance of how your abilities have helped us all today."

"Really?" said Julie.

"Really and truly," said Mashta.

Julie took the claw and bowed. "Thank you."

"Does that thing over there mean it's time to go home?" asked Mr. Hinkle. He pointed.

As the moon finally vanished in the brightening sky, the rainbow stairs shimmered into view. They looked brighter than ever.

"I guess we'd better get back," said Neal. "So we can return ASAP."

Mashta twirled her short staff in the air. "We have much work to do also," she said. "After we restore Koomba, the Sand Children and I will gather bands of folk all across Droon. We must rise up against Gethwing. Jaffa City shall not be burned. We shall win!"

The little folk cheered again.

"We have work, too," said Keeah. She turned to Neal and Julie. "With the fazool, we may find a way to cure Eric. We'll solve Galen's riddle and find the Moon Medallion. In the meantime, Hob, you and I will ride to Zorfendorf like the wind."

"Do what you can for our son," said Mrs. Hinkle, her eyes brimming with tears. "He means everything to us."

Mr. Hinkle placed his arm around his wife and nodded. "We're trusting in you."

Keeah nodded firmly. "I won't fail."

"May Hob add that you are quite legendary," said Hob, bowing to the Hinkles. "It's been a pleasure to know you."

Moments later, Keeah and Hob were riding swiftly across the red sands to Zorfendorf.

As Mashta and her Sand Children

cheered, Julie, Neal, and Mr. and Mrs. Hinkle made their way to the staircase.

Halfway to the top, Julie felt a warm breeze drift across her cheek. It was unlike the desert breezes, and she knew what it meant.

In her mind's eye, she saw a lanky figure run silently across a flat stretch of black ground. It was followed closely by two others just like it. All three had heavy sacks hanging over their shoulders.

"I see the Hunters!" she said.

But . . . where are they?

Searching her vision, Julie realized she knew the place. It was the parking lot of her school. A moment later, the three figures slipped inside the school doors and vanished.

Quickly, she told Neal and the Hinkles what she had seen.

"The Hunters at our school?" said Neal. "Maybe they're still there. Let's go teach them a lesson. Let's give them some kind of detention. Let's expel them!"

"That sounds like a battle," said Mr. Hinkle. "It's lucky we're on the job now. Bob said we're legendary."

"Hob, dear," said Mrs. Hinkle, "and I think he was referring to me. Either way, kids, from now on, we're helping you every inch of the way!"

Julie and Neal shared a look.

Oh, brother! Here we go again!

THE ADVENTURE CONTINUES!

The wizard Galen has been captured! Neal, Julie, and Keeah are desperate to rescue him. They set out to find the only thing that can free him: the famous Ruby Wand.

Unfortunately, the wand has fallen into the paws of Anga, the wily king of the weasels, and he'll do anything to keep it. Magic won't work against the powerful wand, so the kids must use their wits. But how do you trick a trickster?